ctic Journal

by Dr David James Hasick

Standing L to R Mark Maumill *(Radio operator)*, Dave Pottage *(Weather observer)*, Mal Ellson *(Chef)*, Jim Hasick *(Station leader)*, Paul Fenton *(Plumber)*, Ray Pike *(Construction foreman)*, John Jamieson *(Scientist)*, Brett Backhouse *(Plasterer)*, Paul Gray *(Carpenter)*, Paul Gleeson *(Electrician)*, Philip Cook *(Carpenter)*, Chris Stevenson *(Radio technician)*, David Barrett *(Scientist)*, Trevor Menadue *(Weather observer)*, Steve De Vere *(Camera operator, BBC)*, John Toms *(Diesel mechanic)*, Graham Mills *(Plant operator)*, Paul Munro *(Electrician)*

Kneeling L to R Tim Gibson *(Diesel mechanic)*, Mark Conde *(Scientist)*, Christine McConnell *(Medical officer)*, Al Rooke *(Radio operator)*, Richard Roy *(Radio technician)*, Arthur Gillard *(Diesel mechanic)*, Andy Cramond *(Weather observer)*, John Hoelscher *(Electrician)*, Dave Cesar *(Diesel mechanic)*, Kev Sheridan *(Carpenter)*, Randall Bridgford *(Plumber)*

MAGIC BEAN IN-FACT

Dear Reader,

During 1991-92, I led an expedition of thirty people to Mawson station in Antarctica. Throughout this expedition I kept a journal. This book is based on my journal.

Our tasks included studying the weather, windspeeds and the penguin population; replacing and maintaining buildings, and making a television documentary. As leader I made sure that we had a safe, happy and productive community.

Antarctica is a place of extremes. The windspeed changed rapidly from 0-200 km/h; the temperatures near Mawson ranged from -50 to +6 degrees Celsius. There are times, in December, when the sun is always visible, but in June there are times when it can not be seen at all.

During the month of March the sea around us froze to a thickness of nearly two metres, and blocked the way for ships to arrive until the following November. Communication with the rest of the world had to be by fax, telex or telephone. Our group was alone for nine months. There was no way out.

We had to take enough food, fuel, clothing and building materials to last us twelve months. We had to melt ice to make fresh water for drinking, cooking and washing, and we had to make our own electricity. We were so isolated, that people had to have extra skills. Some people were trained to help the doctor in case an operation was needed. Others were trained in firefighting.

My photographs and journal entries will give you some idea of the excitement and wonder I felt at being an expeditioner in the harsh and extreme environment of Antarctica.

Jim Hasick

Jim Hasick
January 1993

Date: Sunday, 1st December, 1991
Temperature: 20°C.
Weather: A fine day with light winds.
Location: Hobart, Australia.

Today we sailed on the ice-ship 'Aurora Australis'. After many months of training and packing stores at the Australian Head Office in Hobart, we finally began our 6,000 km journey to Mawson, Antarctica.

As we waved goodbye to many friends and relatives who lined the dock, we knew

Tearful farewells as we depart

we would not see them for at least twelve months. We threw streamers to the waving crowd as the ship slowly pulled away from the dock. We even had a band to farewell us.

Date: Tuesday, 3rd December, 1991
Temperature: 12°C.
Weather: Windy with some cloud.
Location: Southern Ocean, about
850 kilometres from Hobart.

The 'Aurora Australis' is pounding through rough seas in the Southern Ocean. Not many expeditioners to meals today due to sea sickness!

View from the bridge

Date: *Sunday, 8th December, 1991*

Temperature: *3°C.*

Weather: *An overcast day with slight breeze.*

Location: *Southern Ocean, about*
           2,800 kilometres from Hobart.

A lot of excitement today as we sighted our first iceberg. Later in the day we saw another huge iceberg, which we estimated to be several kilometres long and about 30 metres above the sea level.

Cameras click as we pass an iceberg

Date: *Friday, 13th December, 1991*

Temperature: *-5°C.*

Weather: *Sunny day with light winds.*

Location: *Mawson station, Antarctica.*

10 a.m. The 'Aurora Australis' is locked firmly into sea-ice 40 km off the Mawson coast. We flew into Mawson using three helicopters.

3 p.m. We flew some scientists to a mountain range 20 km from Mawson.

3.15 p.m. One of the helicopters landed too hard on the crusty snow surface and rolled over. The helicopter was badly damaged but no one was hurt.

4 p.m. We all returned safely to Mawson in the two remaining helicopters.

What a mess! A lucky escape.

Date: Tuesday, 17th December, 1991

Temperature: -6°C.

Weather: A glorious day with blue skies, no wind.

We had a barbecue outside in the sunshine to mark our first day in charge of Mawson station. We had 77 people at Mawson, although only 30 of us would stay here for the whole year. The rest are scientists and trades-people who will return to Australia in March.

Making camp at Bechervaise Island

2 p.m. Some scientists skied 3 km on the sea-ice to spend the night on Bechervaise Island, where they will study the Adélie penguins that nest there. 3 p.m. We sent a helicopter to carry food supplies to the island.

8 p.m. I asked everyone at Mawson to come to a meeting so that we could talk about safety and the work we would be doing during the year.

10 p.m. I talked on the two-way radio to the expeditioners on Becher-vaise Island. They were all well and will be return-ing to Mawson tomorrow.

Making the most of the helicopters

7

Date: Wednesday, 25th December, 1991

Temperature: -5°C.

Weather: Another bright, clear morning with a little more breeze than we have been used to.

The field party who went to photograph the midnight sun from Mount Henderson returned this morning.

4 a.m. A group of 'minstrels' visited all the sleeping areas singing Christmas carols and wishing everyone a Happy Christmas.

10 a.m. We had a special chicken breakfast. Soon afterwards, Santa arrived with a gift for everyone.

Plenty of fun on Christmas Day

3 p.m. Christmas dinner. Christmas messages were received by radio telegram from friends and relatives and from other Antarctic stations. An excellent day!

Date: New Year's Eve, 1992

Temperature: 2°C.

Weather: Bright day with slight wind.

A very busy day. Discussed field training program for expeditioners. Held a fire drill at noon. Improved our communication skills using two-way radios. The Club is being changed into a 'disco' for a New Year's Eve party.

Date: *Wednesday, 8th January, 1992*

Temperature: *-3°C.*

Weather: *A beautiful day. No wind. Blue skies.*

Location: *10 km south of Mawson.*

We are practising safe methods for travelling in Antarctica — how to use tents and cook inside them, how to navigate using map and compass, how to rope together when walking in crevassed country, and how to get out of a crevasse using ropes and special equipment.

Paul 'Cyril' Munroe
doing important training
in case of an emergency

Date: Sunday, 26th January, 1992
Temperature: -1°C.
Weather: Bright, clear morning
                  with a little wind.

10 a.m. Six of us left Mawson to fly 400 km by helicopter to the Prince Charles Mountains. The purpose of the trip was to meet another group of scientists who were based there and to bring back two D7 Caterpillar tractors and sleds, that make up a tractor train.

Part of the tractor train

Cheerful companions

2 p.m.
Location: The Prince
                  Charles Mountains.
Temperature: -20°C.
Weather: Fine with clear skies.

Arrived at the Prince Charles Mountains and joined the scientists for a meal in one of their huts.
4 p.m. We saw the work the scientists were doing on rocks, the icecap and weather. Stayed overnight.

The great, white 'desert'

Date: *Thursday, 30th January, 1992*

Temperature: -18°C.

Weather: A beautiful day with blue skies and no wind.

Location: 300 km south of Mawson.

Travelling with the tractor train back to Mawson from the Prince Charles Mountains. Passing spectacular mountain ranges with steep, snow-covered sides. My birthday today! My companions have made a cake for me. What a privilege it is to be able to spend my birthday in surroundings as spectacular as this.

Date: Friday, 31st January, 1992

Temperature: -20°C.

Weather: Windier and overcast today. Some blowing snow.

The blowing snow is making it hard to see what is ahead. We can't see whether the ice we are travelling on is free of crevasses.

1 p.m. We ran into an area of deep crevasses but fortunately stopped in time.

2 p.m. We checked the area for a safe path.

4 p.m. Continued to Mawson on a track away from the crevasses.

Date: *Wednesday, 5th February, 1992*

Temperature: *-4°C.*

Weather: *Cloudy with some wind.*

Location: *40 km south of Mawson.*

6 p.m. One of the D7 tractors broke a track. This is a big setback and a difficult repair to make. I radioed Mawson to ask the mechanics to bring some extra tools to us.

8 p.m. The mechanics arrived with the tools, and work began to repair the broken track.

12 a.m. Still working on the track. I made hot drinks and a snack.

2 a.m. Job completed. We head for the sleeping vans on the tractor train.

John Toms hard at work

Date: *Thursday, 6th February, 1992*

Temperature: *-3°C.*

Weather: *Another cloudy day with some wind.*

Returned safely to Mawson with tractor train.

Winter freeze sets in

Date: *Friday, 13th March, 1992*

Temperature: *-12°C.*

Weather: *A little cloudy and*
           almost no wind.

The sea has begun to freeze. Some 'pancake' ice has formed in the harbour.

13

Will we see this ball again?

Date: Friday, 17th April, 1992
Temperature: -19°C.
Weather: Snow falling. It is most unusual
*   to see huge snow flakes (about*
*   1cm across) falling in Antarctica.*

Today is a fun day! Hot cross buns for morning tea, then a barbecue lunch before a sea-ice carnival! The sea-ice is now 36 cm thick, so we can safely walk and ski on it.

The first activity is tunnel-ball; then a cross-country, ski race; a dog-sledging race; golf-driving competition and tug-o-war. A top day. Weather improving to blue skies and no wind by the end of the afternoon.

Date: Thursday, 23rd April, 1992
Temperature: -20°C.
Weather: A fine day with slight wind.

Phone link-up with Australia to celebrate the 80th birthday of Dr Philip Law, the founder of Mawson station. He set up the station in 1954 and it has operated continuously since then. I made a speech by telephone to a large number of people gathered to honour Dr Law. I said that although some things like communications, having television and modern buildings had changed at Mawson, the traditions of working closely together, and the mid-winter celebrations, had remained the same.

Date: *Wednesday, 13 May, 1992*

Temperature: -13°C.

Weather: Clear skies and slight wind.

10 a.m. Spoke to field party by radio. They were a little cold but well. They are at the weather station 180 km inland from Mawson. Temperature there was -50°C and the wind speed 20 km/h.

Brrr! What a job!

Date: Tuesday, 19th May, 1992

Temperature: -23°C.

Weather: A clear day with slight wind.

Chef is out on a field trip, so I baked the bread today. The loaves turned out OK!

Come and get it!

Date: Saturday 6th June, 1992

Temperature: -24°C.

Weather: Cold day with clear skies, no wind.

The sun has been getting lower and lower on the horizon each day. Now we cannot see it at all. Just have an orange glow on the northern horizon at midday and then it is dark for the rest of the day.

Mal busy in the kitchen

After lunch everyone did station duties — cleaning inside the buildings, taking waste from the kitchen to the incinerator and measuring the thickness of the sea-ice. Today the sea-ice was 1 metre thick. We played bingo and chess in the evening.

Date: Sunday 21st June, 1992

Temperature: - 7°C.

Weather: Slight breeze, clear skies.

Mid-winter's Day — a very special day when the sun is at its

Drilling the ice

lowest in the southern sky. After today it will start to get brighter. We were going to have a fireworks display today, but it is too windy.

3 p.m. We had a wonderful feast and then in the evening a big party with songs, poems and even a performance of the pantomime 'Cinderella'. On all the Australian Antarctic stations, it has been traditional to do this pantomime on mid-winter's day. A great day.

16

Date: *Tuesday 30th June, 1992*

Temperature: -12°C.

Weather: Calm with clear skies.

We found out today (by satellite telephone from the Antarctic Head Office) that the husky dogs are to be sent from Mawson to Ely, Minnesota in the USA. It has been decided, as part of an international agreement, that all introduced species must be removed from the continent by April 1994. Some expeditioners are very upset at losing the dogs. Others think the dogs will have a better life in Minnesota. They will continue to be used as work dogs, pulling sleds. We will make full use of the dogs until they leave in November.

Faithful friend

Date: *Monday, 7th July, 1992*

Temperature: -18°C.

Weather: Clear skies and no wind.

I saw the sun today, for the first time since mid-June. It just showed itself above the northern horizon at midday. What a wonderful sight! The days will start to get longer and warmer now. It is a great feeling to see the orange disc of the sun once again. One can understand how people in ancient times used to worship it!

At last — the sun!

Date: *Tuesday, 14th July, 1992*

Temperature: -21°C.

Weather: Clear, bright day with slight wind.

Travelled to Auster penguin rookery. Estimated about 8,000 emperor penguins there. Most of the birds were carrying eggs or newly-hatched chicks on their feet.

Date: Thursday, 16th July, 1992

Temperature: -27°C.

Weather: Cold morning but no wind. Clear skies.

We decided that two expeditioners will go with the huskies to Minnesota. They will stay for three months to help them settle into their new homes and teach the new dog-handlers about our Mawson dogs.

The last pups in Antarctica

Date: Monday, 10th August, 1992

Temperature: -24°C.

Weather: Clear skies with slight wind.

Scientists talked about their plan to attach a small radio transmitter to the back of an emperor penguin, so that it can be tracked when it goes out to sea to feed.

Two field parties out today. One group is out with two dog teams for five days and Steve is at Auster rookery filming the penguins. I spoke to both groups on the radio and they are well. Three pups were born to Cocoa today.

"Comfortable down there?"

19

Date: Saturday, 15th August, 1992
Temperature: -22°C.
Weather: Overcast with slight wind.

Had a competition to name the new pups. The winning names for the pups were Frosty, Cobber and Misty.

Date: Tuesday, 25th August, 1992
Temperature: -23°C.
Weather: A very nice day. Calm with blue skies.

Helped at the 'melt lake'. Used a heated 'bell' to melt ice, to make water. The pumps had stopped working and the pipes carrying the water to the station had frozen. A slow and cold job getting it all working again.

Some expeditioners are craving certain foods that we have not had for many months — fresh salads, fresh fruit and fresh milk. I would like a hot curry!

20

Date: Thursday, 3rd September, 1992

Temperature: -18°C.

Weather: Fine and calm.

Made a journey to Auster rookery with Al. The emperor penguin chicks had grown since my last visit. Most stayed on their parents' feet or walked around close by.

"Go and find your parents"

Who is being watched here?

Date: *Friday, 18th September, 1992*

Temperature: *-29°C.*

Weather: *Some blowing snow but clearing.*

Al, Dave, Mark and Paul departed Mawson with two nine-dog sledging teams to make a 300 km journey on the sea-ice to the emperor penguin rookery at Kloa Point. Many expeditioners waved them farewell. Steve and Chris filmed the departure of the teams.

Date: *Friday, 9th October, 1992*

Temperature: *-22°C.*

Weather: *Windy morning with blowing snow.*

Travelling with four expeditioners to Fold Island. Met the Kloa dog runners on their way back.

Getting the feel of real Antarctica

Date: *Saturday, 10th October, 1992*

Temperature: *-20°C.*

Weather: *Some wind and drifting snow.*

Location: *Fold Island*

     Made camp at Fold Island for the night. The dog runners counted 1,600 emperor penguins at Kloa. The population has increased from previous years.

8 p.m. Radio message that a tractor train coming down the steep ice slope near Mawson got out of control and two sleds turned over. No one was injured.

Using time lapse photography to capture moonlight at the camp site

Date: *Tuesday, 27th October, 1992*

Temperature: -14°C.

Weather: Some wind (about 15km/h) and clear skies.

Chris, Christine and I caught, weighed and released 27 Adélie penguins as part of a science project.

Weighed and marked...

...all in the name of science

24

Date: *Saturday, 31st October, 1992*

Temperature: -8°C.

Weather: *A real Mawson blizzard! Maximum wind speed*
       180 km/h (105 knots) with blinding, drifting snow.
       This is our highest wind speed this year.

Weather is so bad, I suggest a free day for all who do not need to be at work. There is a deafening roar of the wind and pictures are shaking on the walls. It feels as though the building might be blown away and some expeditioners are quite anxious.

Radio message from the 'Aurora Australis' en route to Mawson. It is 300 km from Mawson and experiencing the same bad weather.

One of our vehicles is almost completely buried by snow.

Who's going to dig this out?

Date: *Monday, 2nd November, 1992*

Temperature: *-7.5°C.*

Weather: *Much lower wind speeds than the last three*
             days but still overcast. It is a relief to be rid of
             the 100+ km/h wind speeds and driving snow.

'Aurora Australis' is expected to berth at the ice edge about 60 km from Mawson. This will mean we will see some new faces — the first for nine months. 11 a.m. The first helicopter from the 'Aurora Australis' arrived! At last some fresh fruit, salads and vegetables — the first we have seen since March. We also received our first letters and parcels from friends and relatives.

Date: *Wednesday, 4th November, 1992*

Temperature: *-7°C.*

Weather: *Overcast and a little windy.*

8 a.m. The huskies were taken to the ship for their journey to Minnesota. The dogs ran the 60 km to the ship but the three pups flew out by helicopter. It is sad to be losing the Mawson huskies. We hope that they are going to a better home in Minnesota and will be happy there.

A film crew is making a film called 'The Last Husky".

Pene Greet, a summer expeditioner, explained her science project to me. She is measuring winds in the upper atmosphere.

An expert at work

Antarctica's last huskies

Date: Thursday, 5th November, 1992
Temperature: -12°C.
Weather: Some high cloud and a little wind.

The arrival of scientists and tradespeople on the 'Aurora Australis' has increased our population from 30 to 67. Some scientists have gone to work at the Adélie penguin project on Bechervaise Island.

Date: Monday, 16th November, 1992
Temperature: -8°C.
Weather: A brilliant day with blue skies and
very little wind. Mawson at its best!

Took two new expeditioners to the emperor penguin rookery at Auster, 50 km from Mawson. The emperors are so majestic. We travelled in a tracked vehicle called a Hagglunds.

Many photographs were taken, including some of myself practising karate in bare feet on the ice. I didn't really feel the cold on my feet until I stopped and then I rushed to get my socks and shoes back on! We also photographed some Adélie penguins and Weddell seals nearby. A wonderful and memorable day.

Kicking to stay warm

"It's your
turn to get
the food."

Catching a little sun

"That was
MY stone!"

Date: *Wednesday, 9th December, 1992*
Temperature: *-7°C.*
Weather: *Another excellent day with blue skies and no wind.*

A Russian tourist ship, 'Kapitan Khlebnikov', arrived 60 km from Mawson. They asked permission for fourteen passengers from America, Australia and New Zealand to visit our base. I agreed.

Date: *Thursday, 10th December, 1992*
Temperature: *-7°C.*
Weather: *A glorious day with blue skies and no wind.*

My last day of this expedition at Mawson. The 'Aurora Australis' has returned and my expeditioners and I will depart for Australia.

Although we are sad to be leaving Mawson, we are looking forward to seeing our friends and relatives again.

2 p.m. We had a barbecue lunch. I thanked all expeditioners for their good work, then I handed the station over to the new Station Leader.

Date: *Sunday, 27th December, 1992*
Temperature: *22°C.*
Weather: *A sunny, warm day.*
Location: *Hobart, Australia.*

'Aurora Australis' arrived back in Hobart.

Happy reunions with our relatives and friends. It is good to see some new faces, green plants and trees, shops and cars. The smell of grass and flowers is very strong.

End note

I thoroughly enjoyed my stay at Mawson. I have many fond memories of my friends, the wonderful scenery and the spectacular wildlife we saw. My funniest memory is of Santa arriving at Christmas. The saddest moment was when the huskies left for Minnesota. And of course, I will never forget that worrying time when the helicopter crashed.

Now, back in Australia, I am enjoying things that people usually take for granted, such as walking in parks, seeing friends and relatives or eating fresh fruit. I have had calls and letters from the Mawson expeditioners. Some are going back to Antarctica on another expedition, as I want to do one day.

I hope that you have seen enough in this journal to make you feel that Antarctica should always be protected.

J.H.

Series Editors Lynne Badger Dip.T., Grad.Dip.Reading Ed., M.Ed.(Hons); Barbara Comber B.A., Grad.Dip.Reading Ed., M.Ed.(Hons); Rodney Martin Adv.Dip.T., B.Ed.

Trialling Teachers Judy Andrews, Immaculate Heart of Mary School, Brompton; Sharon Callen, Pembroke Junior School; Sue Hoare, Kidman Park Primary School.

Photography Owner of title page photograph unknown. All other photographs by the author.

Produced by Martin International Pty Ltd
[A.C.N. 008 210 642] South Australia
Published in association with Era Publications,
220 Grange Road, Flinders Park, South Australia 5025

Text & photographs © James Hasick, 1993
Design and map by Steven Woolman
Printed in Hong Kong
First published 1993
Small book reprinted 1995

National Library of Australia
Cataloguing-in-Publication Data:
Hasick, David James.
      Antarctic journal.

      Includes index.
      ISBN 1 86374 054 6 (big bk.).
      ISBN 1 86374 055 4 (small bk.).

      1. Readers (Primary). 2. Readers — Antarctic regions.
      I. Title. (Series : Magic bean in-fact series).

428.6

Available in:

Australia from Era Publications, 220 Grange Road,
Flinders Park, South Australia 5025
Canada from Vanwell Publishing Ltd, 1 Northrup Cresc.,
PO Box 2131, Stn B, St Catharines, ONT L2M 6P5
New Zealand from Reed Publishing (NZ) Ltd, 39 Rawene Road,
Private Bag 34901, Birkenhead, Auckland 10
Singapore, Malaysia & Brunei from Publishers Marketing
Services Pte Ltd, 10-C Jalan Ampas,
#07-01 Ho Seng Lee Flatted Warehouse, Singapore 1232
United Kingdom from Heinemann Educational Publishers,
Halley Court, Jordan Hill, Oxford OX2 8EJ
United States of America from AUSTRALIAN PRESS ™,
c/- Ed-Tex, 15235 Brand Blvd, #A107, Mission Hills CA 91345